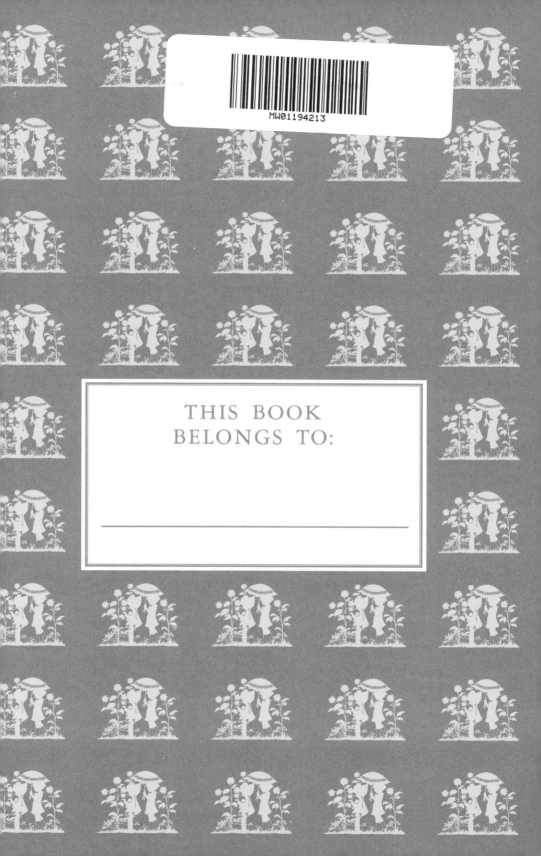

THIS BOOK
BELONGS TO:

_____

MOTHER EARTH'S
CHILDREN

TITLES BY ELIZABETH GORDON AVAILABLE FROM RANDOM HOUSE VALUE PUBLISHING:

BIRD CHILDREN

FLOWER CHILDREN

MOTHER EARTH'S CHILDREN

WILD FLOWER CHILDREN

MOTHER EARTH'S
CHILDREN

THE FROLICS OF THE FRUITS AND THE VEGETABLES

ELIZABETH GORDON
ILLUSTRATED BY M. T. ROSS

DERRYDALE BOOKS
NEW YORK

This 2000 edition is published by Derrydale Books™,
an imprint of Random House Value Publishing, Inc.,
280 Park Avenue, New York, New York 10017.

Derrydale Books™ and design are trademarks of
Random House Value Publishing, Inc.

Random House
New York • Toronto • London • Sydney • Auckland
http://www.randomhouse.com/

Printed and bound in Singapore

Cover design by Sandra Wilentz

ISBN 0-517-16358-6

8 7 6 5 4 3 2 1

This little book is a thank-offering to the thousands of little friends who have so loyally given me their best in the way of encouragement and appreciation, and is most especially inscribed to Gladys Doris.

FOREWORD

A seed, little friends, is really a plant or a tree all wrapped up in a little brown bundle. If you plant it in the ground it will grow, and when it is old enough it will bear fruit, because God has made it so.

Among all the children of Mother Nature, the fruits and vegetables are probably the most useful to us. Wherever we may go some of these little people are there before us, ready to help us by giving us food and to make life easy and joyous for us.

In your Mother's garden you will always find many familiar friends; in the fields the graceful Grain children will nod and beckon to you; in the orchard the Fruit children will peep out at you from their leafy homes; along the roadside the little Berries will give you a friendly greeting; and in the forest you will find the little wild Grapes climbing trees and playing hide and seek with the Bird children.

The publishers, who have also given you the Flower Children, Bird Children, and Wild Flower Children, wish to join the author and the artist in their hope that these new comrades will fascinate and delight you.

For myself, little friends, I thank you from my heart.

ELIZABETH GORDON

LITTLE Miss Radish, pretty thing,
  Has her birthday in the spring;
  She and the little Onions play
  Out in the garden all the day.

WHEN Orchard Oriole sings his song
The Rhubarb children troop along;
They're hardy, healthy youngsters, too,
And stay the whole, long summer through.

SAID Lettuce, tender-hearted lass:
"Come Dandelion, 'neath my glass;"
But Dandelion smiled and said
She liked the nice fresh air instead.

11

SAID Spanish Onion: "I don't see
Why people weep at sight of me;
I'm a nice, friendly sort of chappie
And like to make everybody happy."

THE Button Mushrooms went to play
With the small Puff Balls one bright day;
They had such heaps of glorious fun,
But all ran home at set of sun.

ASPARAGUS in early spring
Came up to hear the robins sing;
When she peeped out her dress was white;
It turned green in the sunshine bright.

THE Green Pea children went to sail
On the Sauce Pan ocean in a gale;
"This boat's a shell," they cried; "Dear me!
We might capsize in this deep sea."

SAID Spinach: "In my dress of green
I'm just as happy as a queen.
I'm truly glad that I am good
For little babies' early food."

LITTLE Wild Strawberry came down
   To visit with her folks in town;
   She's a sweet child with charming ways,
   And blushes modestly at praise.

SAID Endive: "I was born in France
But travel when I get a chance."
Said Celery: "I travel, too,
But my real home's in Kalamazoo."

THE Carrot ladies love to go
To church on Sundays in a row;
And, tall or short, each lady fair
Wears a green feather in her hair.

PEARL Onion, tiny little thing,
Lives out doors from early spring;
She's German, so I understand,
And dearly loves her father-land.

THE dainty little Water Cresses,
In their pretty bathing dresses,
Like water fairies splash and play
In the cool brooklet all the day.

"CHERRIES are ripe," said Old Blue Jay
  As he flew by one August day;
   "Why, he means us," the Cherries cried,
   "Perhaps we'd better go inside."

WHEN Gooseberry wears a gown of green
She cries and pouts and makes a scene;
But when her gown's a purplish hue
She never disagrees with you.

23

THE String Beans love to climb a pole,
And so their clothes are seldom whole.
Mother Bean said: "I'll mend the tatters;
While they are happy, nothing matters!"

SAID Dame Potato: "Hurry, Pat!
And wash your face and feed the cat,
Then run to school, or you'll be late;
Just see!   It's nearly half past eight!"

"GOOD morning, friends! Know who I am?
    I'm Raspberry who makes the jam;
      You know—that on the pantry shelf—
      I make that every year myself."

WHITE Turnip said: "I'm pale, I know,
And all our family are so."
"I should advise," said old White Beet,
"A course of sugar cakes to eat."

RED Pepper said a biting word
Which Miss Green Pepper overheard;
    Said she: "Hot words you can't recall;
    Better not say such things at all."

28

SAID Miss Cucumber: "I have brought
My fan, because the day is hot;
Our family have a splendid rule,—
Whatever happens, we keep cool."

MISS Parsley raised her plumy head,
And in her modest manner said:
"I'm only asked to dine, I know,
Because my dress becomes me so!"

GUMBO'S a splendid southern cook,
And, without looking in the book,
He'll make a savory soup or stew,
And send it, steaming hot, to you.

THE Blueberry children love to run
Around the hillsides in the sun;
Smiling and jolly, plump and sweet,
Best-natured youngsters one could meet.

"EVERY one knows," said Madame Beet,
  "My disposition's very sweet;
    And though to plumpness I am prone,
    My color's every bit my own."

33

"MY new spring dress," said Chicory,
"Is just as lacy as can be;
Shading from green to purest white
Its ruffles are my heart's delight!"

FIG is the queerest chap; you know
The way that fellow starts to grow?
Just a small bud upon the bough,
No flower at all—that's clever now!

THE pretty little ladies Rice
You'll always turn to look at twice;
They came from India long ago,
And now they're everywhere you go.

36

THE Currant ladies look so sweet
In their green dresses, cool and neat.
They offer you, for your delight,
Their strings of berries, red and white.

SAID Brussels Sprout: "I am so glad
That I'm such a good-looking lad."
Horseradish said: "I'm glad I'm plain
If good looks make a chap so vain."

SAID Rutabaga Turnip: "Wow!
I just escaped that hungry cow;
I jumped behind a great big tree
Or she'd have surely eaten me!"

THE Blackberry children love to run
And play beneath the August sun
Until each little maid and man
Takes on a friendly coat of tan.

CARRAGEEN makes his bow to you.
He's a sea child, that is true,
But he's so jolly—never cross—
His other name is Irish Moss.

41

"THE person they named after me,"
Said Oyster Plant, "lives in the sea;
I'm very sure I could not sleep
'Rocked in the cradle of the deep.'"

YOUNG California Artichoke
Exclaimed: "It is the richest joke
That many people, young and old,
How to eat me must be told!"

"DEAR me!" Madam Muskmelon said,
"Those children will not stay in bed;
Before the darlings get misplaced
I'll tie each baby to my waist."

44

WATERMELON'S dress of green
Trimmed in rose pink you all have seen;
She has such pleasant smiling ways,
We welcome her on summer days.

OLIVE'S a sweet Italian maid,
Her gown is green—a lovely shade.
Though just at first she's rather shy,
You get to like her by and by.

THE Mustard Children grew so tall
They looked right over the garden-wall;
They're rather sharp and forward, so
That's why they're left outside, you know.

SAID Cauliflower: "I used to be
A cabbage, so some folks tell me;
When I've improved some more—who
    knows?
Maybe I'll be a Cabbage Rose."

H AND in hand with summer comes
The happy family called the Plums,
Some dressed in purple, some in red;
They're very pretty and well bred.

SAID Garlic: "My home used to be
In far-off, sunny Sicily;
But people here think I'm a blessing,
I make such splendid salad dressing."

50

YAM really is a pretty fellow,
  Though his complexion's rather yellow;
  When Winter comes he packs his grip
  And goes north for a little trip.

SAID pompous, purple Egg-plant: "Well!
So that is egg in that queer shell;
Really! It's very hard to see
Why they named that chap after me!"

V EGETABLE Marrow liked to tell
    How he was once an English swell;
    Summer Squash laughed and said: "My
        word!
    That's quite the best thing Hi 'ave 'eard."

SAID Hubbard Squash: "All summer long
I'm on the farm where I belong,
But in the fall, for change of air,
I go to see the County Fair."

SAID busy, bustling Mrs. Quince:
    "I never have a moment since
    The jelly-making time is here;
    We're making such a lot this year."

SAID Mother Pear: "Dear me! Those twins
Are just as much alike as pins;
 I must do something, I declare!"
 So she cut little sister's hair.

B ANANA wears a yellow coat
Buttoned quite snugly 'round his throat.
He comes from where it's warm, you see,
And feels cold more than you or me.

HERE'S an odd child named Cashew—
Provides you nuts and apples, too;
Oil and wine, and other things
This busy young Brazilian brings.

58

A FOREIGN lady of renown—
Pomegranate in her crimson gown,
Smiling and nodding as she goes,
Looks like an Oriental rose.

LITTLE Miss Sugar Cane is sweet—
In truth, she's good enough to eat.
 She gives us sugar, nice and white,
 And syrup to make things taste right.

H ERR Burgomaster Cabbage said:
"My little dog, he needs some bread."
Frau Cabbage smiled; "Just help yourself,
A fresh loaf's on the pantry shelf."

H ERE'S Apple, loved by young and old
And sometimes worth his weight in gold.
We hail him with delighted cries
When he comes to us, baked in pies.

PINEAPPLE has so many "eyes"
You cannot take him by surprise;
He's full of sunshine, through and through,
And always has a treat for you.

COFFEE said: "I must really study
To find why my complexion's muddy.
Perhaps it's only tan, you know
I do run out bareheaded so!"

M R. Green Tea comes from Japan,
He's such a wrinkled little man;
He says: "My tea is very nice,
Will you have sugar, milk or ice?"

B ARLEY'S a bearded gentleman,
He wears a suit of golden tan;
    Though he has homes both east and west
    He loves the prairie lands the best.

"I DINNA care," said bluff Scotch Oat,
   "For dinner at a table d'hote;
   A bowl of porridge and some tea,
   At home, are good enough for me."

"I'LL be grown up," said Caraway,
  "And out of school Thanksgiving Day;
   That's a good thing, too, 'cause you see,
   They can't make cookies without me."

68

"OUR family's not hard to suit,"
Said Mrs. Peach. "We're simple fruit;
We like most any kind of weather
If the sun shines, and we're together."

H ICKORY Nut looks rough and rude,
Although at heart he's very good.
If once you get inside his shell
You're sure to like him very well.

SAID Cactus: "On the desert wild
I used to be a naughty child,
But since I went to Burbank's school,
I'm good, and live by Golden Rule."

71

"THE boys all call me 'Nigger Toe,'"
Brazil Nut said; "I think I'll go
Back to Brazil; 'twould serve them right
And teach them to be more polite."

COCOANUT has a funny face,
Eyes, nose and mouth all in one place;
He's always busy selling milk,
While Mrs. Cocoanut makes silk.

73

SAID Mrs. Peanut, in a flutter,
 "I quite forgot to salt the butter;"
  The little Peanut children said:
  "Why then, Mama, we'll salt the bread."

SAID Chestnut: "I work for my living,
I stuff the turkey on Thanksgiving.
On winter days I work down town;
You'll know me by my coat of brown."

PERSIMMON said: "I'm up so high
I can reach out and touch the sky."
Bre'r Possum said: "Don't reach too far,
You might put out a shining star."

SAID Mr. Gourd: "You'll plainly see
We are a busy family;
  We give you bottles, cups and things,
  And curly vines for playtime rings."

LITTLE, wise, home-loving Truffle
  Never lets his temper ruffle;
    His home is just beneath the ground,
    And there he always may be found.

MOTHER EARTH'S CHILDREN

WILD Grape just loves to run away
And in the green woods climb and play;
You'll know him when among the trees
His fragrant blossoms scent the breeze.

79

THOUGH Miss Grape Fruit is very young
Her praises are on every tongue;
And though she travels everywhere
She has a very modest air.

80

THE Lemons every summer go
In groups to see the Wild West Show;
Come rain or shine, they never stay
At home on any circus day.

M ISS Cotton is a fairy queen
In her white dress all trimmed with green;
To other children everywhere
She sends such pretty clothes to wear.

M ISS Orange said: "I'd like to know
Those pretty mountain girls called 'Snow;'"
"Don't," said her Dad, "or we are lost;
They're relatives of Sir Jack Frost."

M ISS Beechnut wears a pretty bonnet
With little fuzzy feathers on it.
She's very sweet, and always good;
Her home is in the deep, wild wood.

"I WORK," said genial Mrs. Wheat,
"To give the world enough to eat;
I'm always happy when there's bread
Enough, so every child is fed."

CITRON is very plump and round,
He likes to roll upon the ground;
  Come rain or shine he's always happy,
  A nice, contented little chappie.

CRANBERRY dearly loves to go
Wading in places wet and low;
She wears soft gowns of dainty floss
Made of the pretty yellow moss.

SAID Indian Corn: "I'm heap rich brave,
Much shiny gold I make and save."
So Squaw Corn went and bought a bonnet,
And a silk gown with tassels on it.

NORTH Wind came whistling by one day
Where the Tomatoes were at play;
It gave those children such a fright
They put their blankets on that night.

THE oddest child—when all is said—
Of those we've met, is St. John's Bread;
He's Spanish, so I've understood,
And makes a food that's very good.

THE Nutmeg children ran away
To tease the cook on baking day.
Said Mother Nutmeg, in surprise:
"Why! Who will spice the custard pies?"

THE Pumpkin children, every one,
On Hallowe'en go out for fun;
With Jack o'lantern and his crew
They find such jolly things to do.

WHEN Jack Frost said: "Now, children all
Go in before the snowflakes fall,"
Parsnip declared he liked the snow
To cover him, and didn't go.

SIR English Walnut, pompous, fat,
Is quite a great aristocrat.
His family is very old;
They lived in Bible times, we're told.

THE Popcorn children are so dear
They stay with us all through the year;
They like to dance in dresses white
Around the open fire at night.

INDEX

Apple	. . . . .	62	Lemon	81
Artichoke	. . . .	43	Lettuce	11
Asparagus	. . . .	14	Muskmelon . . .	44
Banana	. . . .	57	Mustard	47
Barley	. . . .	66	Nigger Toe (Brazil Nut) .	72
Beechnut	. . . .	84	Nutmeg	91
Beet	. . . .	33	Olive	46
Blackberry	. . .	40	Orange	83
Blueberry	. . .	32	Oyster Plant . . .	42
Brussels Sprout	. .	38	Parsley	30
Button Mushrooms	. .	13	Parsnip	93
Cabbage	. . . .	61	Peach	69
Cactus	. . . .	71	Peanut	74
Caraway	. . . .	68	Pear	56
Carrageen	. . .	41	Pearl Onion . . .	20
Carrots	. . . .	19	Persimmon . . .	76
Cashew	. . . .	58	Pineapple . . .	63
Cauliflower	. . .	48	Plum	49
Celery	. . . .	18	Pomegranate . . .	59
Cherries	. . . .	22	Popcorn . . .	95
Chestnut	. . . .	75	Potato	25
Chicory	. . . .	34	Pumpkin	92
Citron	. . . .	86	Quince	55
Cocoanut	. . . .	73	Radish	9
Coffee	. . . .	64	Raspberry . . .	26
Cotton	. . . .	82	Red Pepper . . .	28
Cranberry	. . .	87	Rhubarb	10
Cucumber	. . .	29	Rice	36
Currants	. . . .	37	Rutabaga Turnip . .	39
Dandelion	. . .	11	Scotch Oat . . .	67
Egg Plant	. . .	52	Spanish Onion . . .	12
Endive	. . . .	18	Spinach	16
English Walnut	. .	94	String Bean . . .	24
Fig	. . . .	35	St. John's Bread . .	90
Garlic	. . . .	50	Sugar Cane . . .	60
Gooseberry	. . .	23	Summer Squash . .	53
Gourd	. . . .	77	Tomato	89
Grape Fruit	. . .	80	Truffle	78
Green Onion	. . .	9	Vegetable Marrow . .	53
Green Pea	. . .	15	Water Cress . . .	21
Green Pepper	. . .	28	Watermelon . . .	45
Green Tea	. . .	65	Wheat	85
Gumbo	. . . .	31	White Turnip . . .	27
Hickory Nut	. . .	70	Wild Grape . . .	79
Horseradish	. . .	38	Wild Strawberry . .	17
Hubbard Squash	. .	54	Yam	51
Indian Corn	. . .	88